A TALE OF
TWO MOTHERS-IN-LAW

A TALE OF
TWO MOTHERS-IN-LAW

Patrick Wright

HEINEMANN : LONDON

For Roger and Eva Cowan

William Heinemann Ltd
10 Upper Grosvenor Street, London W1X 9PA
LONDON   MELBOURNE   TORONTO
JOHANNESBURG   AUCKLAND

First published in Great Britain 1983
© Patrick Wright 1983
434 87827 8

Printed and bound in Great Britain by
Redwood Burn Limited, Trowbridge, Wiltshire

THE LONG WEEKEND

THAT SINKING FEELING.

THE ARRIVAL.

THE DAYDREAM.

THE OUTRAGE.

TOGETHERNESS.

THE SPECIAL MEAL.

NEWS AT TEN.

SUNDAY AFTERNOON.

A MOMENT OF MADNESS.

MONOPOLY.

THE BOOBY-TRAP.

THE WORKSHOP.

NIGHTMARE !

THE SIEGE.

HOME SWEET HOME.

A DAY AT THE SEASIDE

THE FAMILY PORTRAIT.

HIGH JINX.

THE EMERGENCY.

THE LONG JOURNEY HOME.

BABYSITTING

THE SUPERGRASS.

OUT AND ABOUT

THE RIVALS.

DINING OUT.

STAMPEDE !

MOTHER'S CONTACT LENS.

THE PARTY

THE FART.

CORNERED!

FAMILY PHOTOGRAPHS.

CHRISTMAS

SOCKS.

THE GIFT.

CARVING THE TURKEY.

THE DEPARTURE.

ABSENT FRIENDS.